THE DRAKONEBORNE SYMPOSIUM

VOLUME I

ISABELLA ROSINANTE

COPYRIGHT

The Drakoneborne is the product of the author's imagination and is used fictitiously.

Names, characters, places, and incidents are loosely based on Greek Mythology and the Middle Minoan Period of 1700 BCE. Any resemblance to actual persons, living or dead, events, or locales is entirely coincidental.

Copyright © 2021 by Isabella Rosinante

Edited by Ana Joldes

All rights reserved.
No part of this publication may be reproduced, stored in a retrieval system, or transmitted in any form or by any means, electronic, mechanical, photocopying, recording, or otherwise, without written permission of the writer. For information regarding permission, visit the website below.

Published in the United States.

Second Edition

The Drakoneborne/Isabella Rosinante. ISBN: 978-1-955266-24-6

www.thedrakoneborne.com

For Mark, who heard this story first,
for Tom, who provided food and shelter during a pandemic,
for Waleed and everyone who battled COVID-19 in the hospital,
and for my readers in Greece, the UK, Germany, France,
and all the distant lands,
who had been waiting for this—thanks a bunch!

CHRONOLOGY

The story you hold in your hands is the first volume. It takes up immediately after the symposium. The book focuses on events in and around Central Southern Crete to pick up the tales of Pylyp, Erythrus, Merope, Theresa, Kyros, and a plethora of characters not yet introduced.

All volumes are told through the limited omniscient point of view of a third person, meaning the yarn spinner only has knowledge of the perspective character's thoughts and experiences for the duration of the storytelling. The viewpoint is subjective, depending on the focal character. However, at times, the narrator may use an authorial omniscient point of view to advance the plot.

The characters come from different backgrounds but weave in and out of each other's lives as they navigate a chaotic world for survival. Some stories cover minutes, an hour, or a day; others might span a fortnight, a month, or half a year. With such a structure, the narrative cannot be strictly sequential; sometimes, important things are happening simultaneously.

Next up, *Killing Fire*.

Isabella Rosinante

PYLYP

A clear day. The whole island of Crete, the Cyclades, and Mount Taygetus in the Peloponnese were in Pylyp's panoramic view.

It's Basilios, he thought. The month that harboured the beginning of disaster and calamity. Basilios was the month of fear. The last month of a dry summer, a period during which fertile plains were threatened with drought. People suffered and starved, depriving the gods of sacrifice and worship. Their anguish could be heard. Those who could would pray, behave, and live honestly to get through the month.

Everyone had heard the old stories of a distraught Goddess Demeter, the goddess of the harvest and agriculture, the giver of food, the law-bringer, the divine order of the unwritten law. She of the grain, who searched high and low for her daughter, Persephone, causing terrible droughts along the way.

Some even said the meteors showering and lighting the sky every year were the goddess's tears, those of a mother who felt separation closing in.

'There is power in the grief of a mother,' his grandfather, Praxilaus, once said.

Pylyp had his concerns, but he did not give them voice. He would probably have heard the exact same words. His grandfather was full of anecdotes of sorts that boasted of wisdom and truth. Praxilaus was a forty-eight-year-old man whose hair and trimmed beard were almost white. His eyes were weary, his face haggard, and his clothes worn out. He stood by Pylyp's side, digging limestone with his bronze-made tools.

Since this was the last month before Persephone's return to the Underworld, this did not make Pylyp feel at ease. Crops would cease to grow, and all the world would have to wait for her return, just like Goddess Demeter, in a wintry state. In his fourteen years, this was his first deep, unsettling feeling. Surrounded by mild frigid conditions on a range of six-thousand-foot-tall mountains, Pylyp saw the sun before the dawn. He took a deep breath, slowly filling his lungs with chilled air from Notus's breath.

Pylyp's attention was drawn to a bearded vulture as it flapped its wings in their direction. He looked up and saw the bird soaring high above, transforming the landscape below into a map of the Amari Valley, with its mountain peaks and unyielding winds. The sun peered through them, and similarly inhospitable landscapes, such as Mount Kedros, were separated by fertile plains that resembled a more civilised world.

The bay was full of working men and women digging through the sun-bleached mountain rocks. The bird of prey swooped down into view and came to rest on Praxilaus's forearm, with a small parchment scroll dangling from its leg. Pylyp watched as Praxilaus removed the scroll and examined the wax seal that featured a teardrop of blood.

'Giants' insignia. Bright orange-reddish glow. Palpable smugness. You must be Scylax!' Praxilaus said in a soft tone, smiling.

Scylax turned his small, feathered head and stared with yellow eyes. The red scleral ring that surrounded them was so luminous, showing how excited he was to be acknowledged.

Everyone in their circle knew who Scylax was. Years ago, an eight-month-old child named Alcaeus strangled a snake in each hand, which had been sent by Goddess Hera to kill him. As a scavenger that flew above Alcaeus when this happened, Scylax descended to eat the dead reptiles.

It was considered a good omen to have a bearded vulture fly over you. With that in mind, Zeus bestowed on him the honour of serving as Alcaeus's watcher. He adorned Scylax's beak and feathers with metal strength to physically protect him from harm and made him resistant to poison.

Scylax looked intimidating but was very tame and a perfectly harmless adult bird. At least when Pylyp did not attempt to touch him. Pylyp remembered the time he admired his fiery appearance and tried to stroke the bird. Scylax would not partake in this behaviour and wounded his fingers with a bite. It took Pylyp two moons to heal.

Scylax had a daily sand bath ritual in secret places to keep his feathers bright. Their orange hue was a symbol of superiority in the knowledge of his surroundings. Praxilaus loved to tell Pylyp that knowledge was power, which was well reflected by this bird that was most proud of it. But in his case, Pylyp always thought the bird was simply at the right place at the right time, and knowledge had nothing to do with it.

Praxilaus broke the seal. His eyes moved over the words.

'Well . . . what does it say?' asked Pylyp.

'Lady Alkmena wants us to postpone our trip by a fortnight.'

Pylyp adored Lady Alkmena, and he would do whatever she asked without objections. She temporarily stayed as a guest with them, hiding away from Goddess Hera. She lived alone with her two sons in the only outdoor structure seen near Idaion Andron Cave. Her face and dark eyes rivalled the Goddess Aphrodite.

Pylyp visualised this tall, beautiful woman with her austere face and couldn't help but feel his heartbeat thundering. He knew he had experienced someone special each and every time. A figure that men would travel miles to see. Scylax and Lady Alkmena had a bond. After all, he was the watcher of her child. But that bond made Pylyp jealous. Pylyp, overwhelmed by her beauty, took a deep breath and preserved her vision in his memories.

As Pylyp drifted off, Praxilaus took notice. 'We are not here for a break, boy. Pick up your tools and do some work, will ya?'

The product of their labour was block-shaped stones, which were then raised high by their communal strength and loaded onto carts.

'If only they used papyrus, we wouldn't have to do all this,' Pylyp sighed. He had no interest in this job.

As Praxilaus's fingertips wrapped around a hammerstone, he dug with all his strength into the unyielding rock. He struck, his aim true. He let out exhaustive chuckles of breaths along the way till the rock finally cracked.

'Engraving true history on unbreakable stones and dispersing them throughout the world is part of who we are. We entrust our knowledge to the future. Our children. Your children.'

Praxilaus took a sharp breath.

'Anyone can write on papyrus. But the message can be destroyed,' he conveyed as he pressed the scroll piece into his palm. 'Remember, boy. Knowledge is power.' He inclined his head, looming over his grandson.

The air suddenly felt heavy. Pylyp's eyes stretched above Praxilaus's shoulder and widened with fear. His eyes reflected a drakon soaring through the skies. The bird of prey peered down with fiery eyes. Frozen and unable to breathe by the sudden appearance of a titan, Pylyp hoped he'd go unnoticed. He felt he could be killed at any time.

That was Titan Iapetus in drakon form. His energy had a tremendous, nasty feel and burnt so intensely that it spread terror in their hearts. Cries rang out as Iapetus soared overhead. Pylyp and Praxilaus stood side by side, their clothing and hair whipped in the wind of Iapetus's wingbeats. A blast of air blew upon their faces as the drakon slowly disappeared, leaving everyone watching in quiet awe.

A heartbeat later, the ground vibrated with a dull, thunderous beat. One calamity after another. Everyone paused in dread, searching for the source of the noise as it slowly increased in frequency and volume.

'What's going on? The mountain rumbles from its plinth! It feels as if it's coming alive!'

'It *is* alive, boy!' Praxilaus said.

Scylax stretched his wings and leapt into the sky. He flew off in no time. Now that there was no drakon in the sky, there was room for one more bird of prey. Watching Scylax's wide aerial, Pylyp saw the mountain was a dormant giant slowly waking up, moving its elbow and scraping the sky.

Pylyp drew in multiple sharp breaths. As the ground beneath him shook with the most vicious of tremors, he forgot how to breathe. He felt that with any heartbeat now, the ground would open to swallow him alive. After a few moments, the vibration and the noise settled. Pylyp fell to the ground, trembling.

Praxilaus placed his arm on his shoulder. 'Are you alright, boy?'

'Am I alright? It's Basilios month!' he exclaimed as he hastily gasped for air. 'Anything is possible. Goddess Demeter causing droughts could kill us all. Titan Iapetus, appearing in rage, could kill us. Standing on an angry giant could kill us all,' he said, his voice loud and squeaky. 'I am totally fine!'

Praxilaus offered a hand to lift him off the ground.

'That which does not kill us makes us stronger. Remember, knowledge is power.'

Familiarity, awareness, and understanding gained through experience, when applied, can make one powerful. Pylyp understood what his grandfather wanted to tell him, but he had no interest in the sentiment. He did not want to be familiar with feelings of fear nor be aware of how powerless he was against the gods. He just wanted to go back to the tavern his mother had left him to run after her death and serve raki and wine to the working men and women of the mountains.

Pylyp was a descendant of a Dactyl and his father's only legacy. That legacy weighed on him, and the tavern work was his solace. He did not want to follow in his father's footsteps and become a healer, nor did he see himself as a copper or blacksmith. He did not want to be there from the very beginning.

Praxilaus's fingertips wrapped around his hammerstone once more, and he dug with all his strength into the unyielding rock. 'Our dull world moves with hazy distortions, and our people are but flickers before their eyes. Some say the giants wake every hundred years to feast but would now wake no more. Not dead at all, I say. Just sleeping. Healing. Renewing. Preparing.' A cruel grin spread across his face. 'Only the presence of powerful deities can stir them to life. Just like that one.'

The sun had barely peeked over the horizon when a frown crossed Pylyp's face.

'I have heard of the giants' deeds, which are told and retold around tavern tables. These stories are the heart and soul of Mount Ida. But I am most certain I am not familiar with the tally against the titans.'

Praxilaus shared his knowledge as he tried to conjure the rock with his hammerstone.

'A billion years ago, chaos birthed Gaia, the Ancient One, the ancestral mother of all life. An enormous feminine being with veins bulging on her temples, a pair of horn-like protrusions extending from either side of her forehead, and a third eye in the centre. An inward energy that is feminine yet dark and negative. She birthed an outward masculine energy, bright and positive . . . Uranus. A divine male being with a ridged, star brass dome depicted over him.

'Their sacred union bore the titans . . . drakons hatched from their Orphic eggs now orbing around as wandering stars. The hecatoncheires came second. They harboured a brass dome on their back that depicted a hundred hands of unfathomable strength, fifty heads over them. They were powerful creatures that brought earthquakes and gigantic sea waves in their wake.

'Then came the cyclopes, giant humanoid creatures with their upper body like copepods, and a million years later, the giants. They were born by a rain of blood at the volcanic Mountain Etna. Tall creatures with skin made of rock, which emerged from the soil within a volcanic eruption. The intense fight among siblings continued for millions of years between the Cretaceous and Palaeogene eras.

'Those constant wars took a massive toll on the land, reshaping it. Legends say the Three Fates helped the titans win the war against the giants in order to put an end to this strife. The titans' power overcame that of their siblings, which they considered a victorious feat. Gaia's children, with whom she shared her powers, lacked a bond. To protect her precious nursery, Gaia gave birth once again . . . to humans, also known as the ancients.

'Born bare, with Nyx their sole witness under the starry sky. Healthy bodies to sustain wholesome spirits and emotions instead of power. They nurtured trust and created bonds. Humans possessed love. Divine deities possessed brute power. Together, they made chaos once more.

'The primordial successors felt superior; some were even disgusted by human weakness. But this world would come to an end if either was annihilated. Power without bounds would bring calamity to the world. A million years later, here we are . . . in this Dark Age because there is nothing left to acknowledge what happened, aside from the inscription on discs and stones written by our ancestors.'

Praxilaus watched his grandson idly listen to the story, making no use of the tools in his hand. 'Now, get back to work, boy. Enough slacking.'

Pylyp had a knack for absorbing information and didn't find digging a waste of time anymore.

ERYTHRUS

Sunlight pierced the leafy canopy of the forest in angled spears of light. Erythrus held a spear while loping through the forest with his king father, Rhadamanthys, who governed Phaestus and the island of Crete.

Erythrus, the king's eldest legitimate son, was a clean-limbed and handsome man with a straight posture, hard muscles, and dark hair. They were on a wild deer hunt, testing the skills of his youngest brother, Gortys, who was well-behaved and dutiful.

The trees stood like centuries-old sentinels. Archers, armoured for hunting, were scattered around them. At least five, perhaps more. Meleagros and Cycnus were among the king's party, both loyal to the crown. Meleagros was the king's familiar, a lean, dark-haired, hard-eyed man whose face was marred by scars. Cycnus, on the other hand, was the king's guard, and his appearance alone gave way to how formidable he was, his entire body designed to commit violence.

Rhadamanthys placed his hand on Gortys's shoulder as he paced towards his target.

'You are hunting, not chasing. Slow down.'

'I think you are getting old, Father.'

Gortys's shoulder blades rippled beneath his skin but did not clench together. Rhadamanthys tested his stance, placing a steady hand beneath his son's drawing arm. Everything fell into place with perfect alignment.

'Very good,' Rhadamanthys whispered.

With a full draw, Gortys's arrow, drawing arm, and body structure melded seamlessly with his target. The arrowhead lay directly beneath his pupil, poised for flight. Gortys pushed his bow forward, and with a graceful motion, the arrow was released.

At the same time, Erythrus drew his spear and launched it with deadly precision at a man in tattered rags who sprinted through the forest, hotly pursued by the king's relentless guard. As the deer fell to the ground, so did the man, both now still and lifeless, their journey's end reached under the watchful gaze of trees. The scents of hunt and blood clung to Erythrus like perfume. Gortys and Rhadamanthys turned their full attention to the fallen man.

In a hasty movement, Rhadamanthys approached the body. Blood stained the grass.

'What is going on?' Rhadamanthys asked.

In the distance, a voice could be heard, that of Cycnus offering his apologies, 'My apologies, Your Grace, for the man has slipped from my grasp.'

The king shifted his unrelenting gaze to Erythrus. 'What have you done?'

'Serving justice.' Erythrus approached the dead body and removed his spear.

'No matter the crime, everyone has the right to a fair trial . . . to be heard like any other accused. As a royal family member, you should be well aware of that.'

'What would you have done? Wait for Cycnus to move his legs?'

'Even I would run if I saw Cycnus from head to toe coming at me!' Rhadamanthys calmly let out the words, suppressing the emerging ire.

'We hunt; we don't chase. Your words.'

'Don't confuse rules of survival with butchering people, boy.'

Erythrus spotted a blood-soaked pouch fastened to the waist of the lifeless man. With a swift motion, he tore the bag from its tether, peeled away the leather string, and let it spill forth its bounty of gleaming gold nuggets.

'This is a man who fled with the gold he stole. In a place like this, any fool who dares run carrying a bag of gold seeks only a short life with a messy death. Why waste breath on a useless hearing?'

Rhadamanthys kept vigilant watch.

'The Three Fates shall decide,' the king said firmly. 'Once you wield a sword, you become a target. The moment you take a life, your kin becomes a target. Vision becomes distorted, twisted by fear and vengeance. Threats to the crown come in many guises. Do not provoke fate, boy. Do not allow yourself to become a savage. Remember, it is wisdom before weapons.'

Cycnus loaded the lifeless body onto his horse when Rhadamanthys whispered a command, 'You know what to do.'

He bowed respectfully before riding off. It was a familiar force of habit, disposing of the corpses left behind by his future king. He would travel to Amyklaion Port before taking a boat to the gulf between the Letoai Isles, where the River Styx flowed, ever-shifting like a crab.

Nothing was more mysterious than the currents of the Styx. It was an ocean of rivers, some swiftly flowing, some slow, and a league from where one drifted at the rate of a mile an hour, another boat would drift two. The only enjoyable part was watching the sun set over a sea that seemed like a sea of boiling gold.

As Cycnus disappeared into the forest, Erythrus was reminded of a story he had once heard from his loyal servant during a previous journey to the gulf's entrance. It was a tale of an oarsman who had been holding a motionless baby wrapped in a tunic when Cycnus had arrived to dispose of a man's dead body. The mother wept as she cursed the heavens, and the power of her grief was palpable. As the deep blue water swallowed the infant's body, it turned back to a brown abyss, indicating beds of dead and rotten marine coral.

In the dark depths of the River Styx, the phosphorescent gleams of passing spirits were swimming towards the gulf's entrance. The reflections dancing on the surface made the entrance resemble the fangs of a wild beast. He recalled Cycnus's description of a 'beautiful but faithless spirit' and wondered what other secrets the river's depths might hold.

As Cycnus recounted the tale, Erythrus imagined the scene vividly. He could picture Cycnus about to drop the body into the sea and then the sudden appearance of Atropos, the Inflexible One, the one who chose the mechanism of one's death. She stood at the edge of the left island by the entrance, her dark feminine figure looming over the scene. Cycnus had described her curly strands of hair framing her youthful face and a long dress covering her golden, bronzed skin. Erythrus sensed that she was there to inspect the funeral practice of the lost soul, and the image sent a chill down his spine.

'I threw a bunch of grapes and said they were a gift for the afterlife as I wished him good luck,' Cycnus recounted to Erythrus. The sea turned purple, and Atropos changed into a phoenix and set herself on fire, her ashes fading away.

Heartbeats later, their party poured through a thousand years of red humus compost lying thick upon the footpath outside the forest. Rhadamanthys and Meleagros spurred their horses forward, with Erythrus and Gortys's horses falling behind while they paced alongside each other. Despite the distance, Erythrus could still hear them.

'Your Grace. Erythrus's victory to the south has increased our navigation and trading opportunities from Berenice Troglodytica along the coast and others along the Horn of Africa, the Persian Gulf, the

Arabian Sea, and even the Indian Ocean, including the southwestern regions of India. Having said that, I believe—'

'Ser Meleagros,' Rhadamanthys interrupted, 'you are my most trusted adviser, and yet . . . at this very moment, you are not being honest with your king.'

'Forgive me, Your Grace.'

'Since he was a young boy, Erythrus had been prone to vicious brawls with older street urchins and shady underbelly thugs, and he had emerged victorious every time. There was no denying the blessing of Zeus upon him, for his physical prowess was unmatched. But what of his human qualities, which are not what one would expect of the future king of Crete? His last victory held major strategic importance for our trading affairs, yet the cost was the lives of countless innocents.

'Casualties in battles are inevitable, but Erythrus's vile nature had resulted in the annihilation of every wife and child of the fallen, calling it mercy when it was nothing of that sort. The Erythraean Sea bore witness to his wickedness, a constant reminder of the atrocities he had committed.'

The sun had paled since noon. As they pressed forward, the acrid scent of decomposing leaves and rotten wood poured into their noses. Erythrus clenched his jaw, his nerves tensing upon hearing his father's words. This dialogue had been a complete bother.

Gortys had also donned a more observant look, holding the reins of his horse as they rode calmly. He looked at his father, his heart pounding faster than usual. His cheeks gleamed with a reddish tint from the moment he looked at his older brother.

'I think it's wise you apologise to Father!' Gortys chewed on his words.

'I promised Mother on her deathbed, before we lost her to your stubborn birth, that I wouldn't be harsh and that I would care for you. However, be very careful with what you tell me to do. I wouldn't mind teaching you to respect my way!' Erythrus's face flashed with anger, with a hint of sibling rivalry.

MEROPE

Golden rays poured into a wild, grape-filled yard near Matala Port. Working men with curly hair picked wild grapes and applied sulphur. Their T-shaped tunics were adorned with woven embroidery along the hem, sides, and shoulder lines, with varying sleeve and skirt lengths. The House of Oenopion commanded respect, for their attire was an expression of equality.

The working women moved with grace, their long hair in ringlets and their dresses fashioned in the bare-breasted style. Though their large hips and tiny waists were accentuated, it was the rhythm of their movements that caught the eye. With skirts in the shape of a bell and V-shaped ruffles, they went about their work, their dresses lifted and clenched in their fists as they tended to the menial tasks at hand. And when it was time to press the grapes, they stepped into the wooden winepresses, flattening the fruit beneath their feet with a fluid motion that spoke of both strength and elegance.

A proud Minoan herself, among those women, appeared Merope. Her hair was straight and the colour of honey, her body young and strong, her skin as tanned as an ivory sandy beach, and her eyes the shape of almonds. She wore a bodice composed of smooth, fitted lace fastened beneath her breasts and with short sleeves that closely fitted her arms.

As she pressed the grapes, she observed her father, Oenopion, and her oldest brother, Talus, engaged in a conversation. They walked side by side towards their tiny mansion nearby. Those sharply defined, large rectangular blocks of stone and ceramic bricks were blurred as the sweat ran down her forehead.

Once again, he goofs on at my expense, she thought.

Talus took aim with his arrows of jest, striking Merope's ideas and tearing apart her best. She recalled the gardenia, wilted and pale. Past its prime, robbed of its might, a sad and sorry state. Despite Talus suggesting watering the poor plant, Merope knew better. It needed power, so she fed it an egg, an act so absurd that Talus laughed. Soon, the gardenia bloomed in full glory, a stunning display of Merope's will and unwavering belief. It became a lesson for Talus in his mocking laughter.

An outburst of laughter escaped them as Merope looked down at her feet. She found solace in seeing grape skins being stripped away, their sweet juices flowing into special basins. The dense canopy of dry reeds shielded her fair skin, while open-top vats of fermented wine drenched her nose with familiar, uncensored, thirst-quenching, and head-turning scents of flirty spices and flavourings such as cinnamon, cloves, cardamom, orange zest, and black pepper. A wizened crone with saggy breasts used a white linen to strain and refuse by the oak barrels.

That's a youngster's job, Merope thought.

Her younger brother, Maron, interrupted her thoughts when he ran towards her and said, 'Merope, quick! The . . . king . . . h-he . . . is here,' while regaining his breath.

Unable to help herself, she cried out, 'I need to clean my feet. Pass me the cloth. Hurry up!'

Assisted by a woman, Merope descended from the winepress and took a seat to soothe her weary feet. Maron's mouth stretched into a smile as he leered at the buxom domestic servant, who was industriously treading grapes beside his sister. His leering eyes betrayed his lustful thoughts as he studied her every move. In turn, the servant's eyes sparkled mischievously, and a hint of a smile danced upon her lips.

Merope's eyes squinted in anger as she snatched the cloth and hit her brother with it. 'What are you looking at?'

'The sweet, supple wines from Crete.' Maron flushed and ran for the front yard as laughter boomed all around.

Heartbeats later, Merope grew closer to the settlement with every step she took. Her eyes trailed off as the king's party approached. She peered over the wooden fence that slumped and weaved around their property. The king's lips widened with a smile as he approached their viridescent yard, sparkling under the sunlight, and the air was rich with the wine's spicy aroma.

He warmly received a smile in return from Oenopion, and when King Rhadamanthys vaulted from his horse, he was given a warm embrace, too. Erythrus gave Oenopion a disdainful, imperious once-over before he dismounted his horse. When his eyes met hers, the gaze triggered a sickness deep inside. He was more interested in her. His eyes followed her, but she did her best to ignore them.

'Welcome to my humble home, Your Grace. To what do I owe the pleasure?' Oenopion said.

Her father was tall and tanned, his cheeks and jaw covered by a dark heavy moustache and a bristly beard, complemented by long dark-brown hair. His face was deeply lined, and his eyes were blue. Merope's mother, Helike, also emerged with her younger brothers.

Melas was a thirteen-year-old skinny boy with dark hair and black eyes, while Euanthes was two years younger, and her little eight-year-old brother, Athamas, looked somehow smaller and more vulnerable. He hid behind his mother's dress at every given social opportunity and found it difficult to interact with strangers.

There was no mistaking they were all kin. Their big, almond-shaped eyes hinted at the relation. Even more so for her older brother, Salagus, who was the last of the high lords to approach. He was a year older than Merope and the dead spit of their father.

'I've come a long way to pay my respects. How are the preparations coming along?' King Rhadamanthys blazed under the sun. He was a man made for enduring the heat.

'Your Grace will be pleased with this year's vintage. God Dionysus has been kind.' Notus's wind swirled around Oenopion as he stood facing his king.

'May I take a sample back to the palace?' inquired Meleagros.

'M'lord, you may have anything you can carry. Salagus, show Ser Meleagros the vineyard,' Oenopion instructed, and Salagus nodded in agreement.

'In truth, I came all the way here to see you before our move to Boeotia. These are promising times for Crete's greatness. Our navigation and trading opportunities are flourishing, and I need good winemakers to spread the knowledge. You are one of the best I've got. The old age of an eagle is better than the youth of a sparrow,' Rhadamanthys said while he glanced about. 'Would you say you love your king? Love him enough to say your silent farewell to the home you laboured to build and move to Chios for me?'

'Move to . . . Chios?'

'Oenopion, I will name you the king of Chios. I need you there.'

'I . . . was not expecting such honour, Your Grace. I don't know what to say.'

'Answer the summons of your king by moving to Chios with your family. And never come back,' Rhadamanthys replied, empowering his voice with demands of duty.

As Merope found the king's behaviour curious, a friendly laughter came from both sides. The king exuded good humour, and her father sighed pleasantly, though moisture glittered faintly in the corners of his eyes. Merope wasn't sure whether these were tears of joy or sadness. Perhaps both.

Oenopion composed himself but spoke dully, 'What about the symposium, Your Grace? We still have preparations to make.'

'Choose someone and place them in charge. I trust your judgement.'

Rhadamanthys took a few steps back and eyed the line of children standing there, his sight travelling over each and halting at Merope.

'Your children are growing so fast and are quite beautiful. They have been blessed with Helike's eyes,' he said as he gazed at her startling beauty, which had caught his attention.

'That is kind of you to say,' Oenopion said.

'How old are you, my dear?' Rhadamanthys asked.

'Seventeen,' Merope replied, her voice caught in a throat gripped by panic, as if she knew where this conversation was headed.

'Any suitors yet?'

Merope wanted to edge her foot backwards with the timidest of steps and retreat, but she could not. She shook her head.

'I have a son who's looking for a bride.' He glanced at Oenopion and said, 'Perhaps it's not too late for our family line to be bound by blood?'

'Bride?' Merope interrupted, as if her life had entered new dark heights. *I am going to die here.* 'If you forgive me, my king. You've chosen the wrong one. I'm not the wifely type for a royal, Your Grace. I— Well, I sleep late. I don't know a thing about housework. My mother says I am a disaster when I cook. And children? I mean, look at these hips. No way!'

she poured out her heart, invoking a quiet chuckle as sweat trickled down her spine.

'None of that matters to me, my lady,' Erythrus stated, alarming her further.

'Really!? Well, what does? I've lots of faults!'

The lines on his face stretched, jaw clenching, the admiration disappearing from his eyes.

'M'lady, our ancestors used to say a lady's armour is her courtesy, and silence is golden. I think you should practise both.' The venom in his voice was thick.

The flash of red warmed Merope's face, along with a smile that defied pleasure. She moved her lips despite her father's stare and whispered to Talus, who stood by her side, 'Talus, requesting permission to kill.'

'Denied,' he whispered back.

Oenopion glanced over at Merope, then glanced away, cheeks reddening. He took a step forward out of embarrassment, intending to give a reassuring shoulder pat or mutter some words to change the bitterness of the moment.

'Your Grace, it would bring me great honour to connect our families as one. But perhaps it would be in your best interest if I were to use the hand of my sweet daughter to seal my successor's loyalty.'

'Who do you have in mind?' asked the king.

'Apollodorus, Your Grace. Staphylous's son.'

'Leaving the grape cluster in the hands of an experienced raki maker is an excellent choice. Very well.'

'Empty words . . . devoid of loyalty,' Erythrus said fervently, clearly annoyed in some fashion. 'Swear by it. If that is your true intention.'

'That will not be necessary,' Rhadamanthys said, dismissing the notion. He threw an ireful stare at the prince.

'It is. These are just empty words. He needs to prove his loyalty to the crown.'

Oenopion had never seen Erythrus so infuriated, yet remaining silent was not an option. This was the future king. 'I swear, making my witness Zeus, the father of gods and men, that I will fulfil, to the best of my ability and judgement, this oath and this contract. Should Staphylous refuse this union, and the future king still wishes Merope as his bride, she will be his to marry. Merope shall remain in Crete with her older brothers until a decision is made.'

Erythrus looked pleased, a sardonic smile forming on his noble features.

'You are a trusted man.' The king patted Oenopion's shoulder, throwing yet another glare in his defiant son's direction.

Assisted by their servants, Salagus and Meleagros arrived with three big jars of wine, and the air grew warm and heavy with the scent, offering a narcotic effect that washed over them like a tide of seduction. As the wine was loaded onto the mounts of their party, each rider mounted their horse.

'I guess this concludes our business here,' said Erythrus, the last to remount his horse.

When the horses and their riders were at a satisfactory distance away from the House of Oenopion, Merope stared after them.

'May his horse stumble, so he falls on his stupid head in his first tilt,' she said, annoyed by what the day had turned to and thrilled that Erythrus was now gone.

'That's just mean! He might become your future husband,' Talus added with a chuckle, stirring emotions to the already dark and bitter taste the young prince had left behind.

As Talus and Merope slowly paced back home, she paused for a moment before saying, 'He told me it would be a courtesy if I shut up. I don't think so! And why did Father promise me to Apollodorus, anyway? He might as well have promised me to his sister Theresa. That would have been more convincing.'

'Shush. Someone might hear you.'

'It's not like it's a secret,' Merope admitted.

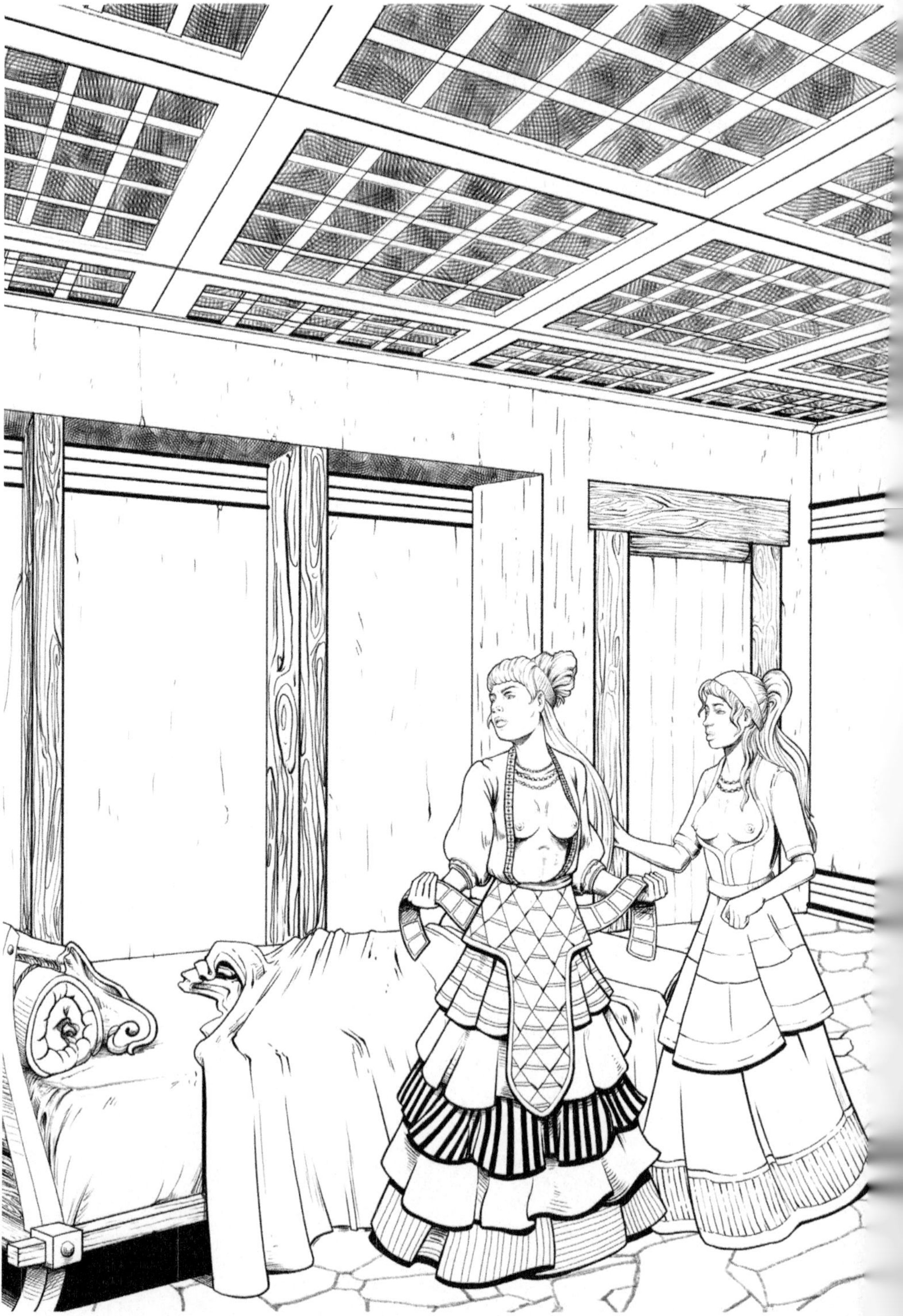

THERESA

Theresa was one of the ancients, like her father and her paternal grandmother and her parents before her. She was a woman blessed with a pretty smile and a certain grace.

She and her brother, Apollodorus, were the legacy of House Staphylous in the south of Crete. House Staphylous kept a godswood, as all the noble houses, but worship was not done at a temple. They had built a small statue of God Apollo in a place where family members and servants alike could walk by and pay their respects and prayers. Worship was for everyone.

She was anointed with oil and the name Theresa, which meant to harvest because she had been born during the Festival of Thesmophoria. A festival held to honour Goddess Demeter.

Her father, however, had always wanted to have a son as his firstborn. As a farmer, he planted his seed, but when Theresa was born, he suffered bitter feelings of disappointment due to *an unsuccessful completion of his harvest*, as he called it. Having felt the gods' judgement, he made a tama to Apollo, his father's brother.

He felt betrayed by his kin. He had prayed for a son and readily offered his son's life to God Apollo in gratitude if his prayer would be answered. Fifteen moons later, his son was born. He was anointed with oil and the name Apollodorus, which meant the gift of Apollo.

Chiore opened the door, followed by Theresa. Of all the rooms in this small wild grape-filled estate near Amyklaion Port, the two of them chose the hallway to fool around. Opposite the statue her father built for God Apollo.

Chiore, a young and giddy woman, served as an apprentice to Theresa. They both dressed in a simple yet elegant style, with affectionate laughter echoing through the air. Beneath their giggles and smiles lay the ever-present risk of getting caught, a sense of adventure that fuelled their excitement. Despite their lighthearted demeanour, Chiore's good heart shone through, a beacon of kindness in the midst of their playful mischief.

Theresa pulled Chiore hard against her and kissed her on the lips, forcing her tongue into her mouth. Chiore licked it with her own tongue, then broke away from her, breathless. Theresa hiked up Chiore's skirt, who leaned back against the wall. Suddenly, she pulled away.

'Not here. Someone might see.'

Theresa shushed her and pointed to her bedchamber up the stairs. Her mother, Demetria, prepared stuffed grape leaves in the kitchen with two domestic servants similarly dressed, not far from where they were. In a hurry, the two women went up the stairs and burst through the door of Theresa's bedroom.

They got very close. Theresa's hand slipped into Chiore's hair. She threw her head back as she kissed her neck. They shared a kiss, and she bit Chiore's lips. Her other hand ran down Chiore's arms slowly and seductively, making her tremble. Theresa then reached between her legs. Chiore took a deep breath, emitting short moans, succumbing.

She smiled, a flush colouring her cheeks. They clawed at each other with a passion exceeding coordination. Chiore responded with equal force and became the dominant one. She took Theresa's dress off, plunged down, and kissed her. She then threw her down on the bed.

Theresa looked up at her straddled. At that moment, Chiore lifted the covers and crawled under them. The ceiling came into Theresa's focus and then lost on Chiore's playful face. Her eyelids closed, shutting the light out. They moved under the covers like a tide.

When they were done, Chiore stood in the shaded sanctuary of closed drapes, smoothing her hair and dressing herself. Meanwhile, Theresa lay in bed with the sheets disarrayed, the memories of their passion still lingering like a sweet perfume. As Chiore returned to the bed, she ran her hands through her hair, lost in the moment's intensity. Theresa turned onto her side, savouring the afterglow of their passion, basking in the warmth of their love.

Chiore lay by Theresa's side, her elbow resting gently on the bed as she traced the curves of her lover's chest with delicate fingers. The skin on Theresa's chest stretched over her sternum, rising and falling with each breath like a dance of passion. Theresa lapsed into a thoughtful silence, and then . . .

'The gods have given us a gift,' Theresa said. 'Brothels.'

'Brothels.' Chiore smiled as if she knew that was true. 'I can think of many other gifts, m'lady. Brothels are not one of them.'

'Married or unmarried, men make no distinctions. But brothels are the reason you don't get raped daily. You get to stay pure.'

'How are you any different?' Chiore said playfully as she trotted forward. 'You make use of me in your bed, take my love and my honour, and you give me nothing but your body.'

Theresa placed her lover's hand over her heart. 'You also have my heart!'

'I am no fit consort for a lady. One day, you are expected to be married, rear a family of your own, and live up to your namesake.'

'I will never be fond of men. I have little love and even less trust in them,' Theresa said in an acid tone. 'But the king is just. Actually, who's worthy enough to judge other than him? If I talk to him and ask his permission, we might be able to—'

Suddenly, Chiore stood up from the bed and interrupted her, 'Please, hold your tongue! What if you shame yourself out there?'

'There is no shame in love.'

A loud knock on the door of her bedchamber made Chiore panic.

'Theresa, are you there?' Apollodorus asked with a chill in his voice.

'Coming.' Theresa scrambled, got off her bed, and dressed with Chiore's help.

'Mother is looking for you.'

She knotted a belt around her waist and replied, 'I am just refreshing myself and changing into new clothes. I will be downstairs soon.'

A few heartbeats later, Chiore opened the door and walked hastily down the stairs. Theresa followed and closed the door. Her brother appeared in front of her—a blond-bearded confronter with intimidating dull eyes, cynicism, and impulses.

'Are you blind or merely stupid? I suppose it amounts to the same thing.'

'Aren't you supposed to be preparing for the symposium?' Theresa ignored him, turning to the heart of the matter.

Apollodorus exhaled as he saw domestic servants walking past. 'Walk with me,' he said, forcefully taking her by the arm and leading her down the stairs. 'As long as Father is assigned as the king's general on the island of Naxos, you are my responsibility. Petulant child! I will tolerate your insolence no longer!'

'Be quick with your words.' Theresa wouldn't tolerate slights coming from her silly younger brother.

'Have you lost your mind whilst lying with a whore?' he asked.

'Her role is to attend to me. I don't know what you are talking about.'

'You bring scandal and ignominy to this house. Don't think I haven't seen you kissing her.'

'We were only kissing. It's not like I am going to marry her,' Theresa finally admitted while adding fuel to the fire with her provocative behaviour.

'If I want, I can doom her to spend the rest of her life sleeping with the swine . . . and to smell like one.'

'Sour grapes, brother?! I think you should try kissing a girl, too. You might like it.'

'You think I've never kissed a girl before?' Apollodorus smiled, but the smile was tinged with arrogance.

As they descended the stairs, Theresa felt the urge to slap the smile off his face but contained herself. She grudgingly bowed and said, 'Then the fate of House Staphylous lies with you, brother.'

'I might invite her to my room tonight and let her make a man out of me. Taste her. See why you are so fond of her.'

'You will forfeit your life in trying.' His words upset her more than she had expected.

Apollodorus grabbed his sister's chest and gave her nipple a tweak. 'Tell me, sister, is she still pink between her legs? Since you've been down there?'

Theresa reacted to the pain inflicted and immediately grasped his crotch between her thumb and forefinger and twisted. 'You should start appreciating what's between your legs, 'cause next time you put your hands on me, you'll have no family jewels left.'

Her brother struggled to remove her hold. 'I will just rip off your manhood and beat you about the head with it . . . *and* you'll never grow another!' Theresa added, before she removed her hand. 'You think of that before you lay a hand on me again.'

Theresa walked past the statue of God Apollo and bid her brother farewell.

KYROS

Kyros stood there in awe, the view in front of him as mesmerising as it was familiar. Though the road to the port market was one he knew well, he could only thank the gods for his good fortune. The sea, a canvas of serenity and commotion, lay stretched before Kyros. Its depths and shallows, painted in hues of ultramarine and sky, presented a mesmerising spectacle against the bustling yet tranquil backdrop. A sunlit sward led upward for a hundred feet or so to where a great rock, the highest point of the Amyklaion Port, stood, casting its shadow in the sunshine.

The rocks, lashed by foam, shimmered in the sunlight as the Libyan Sea approached, calm and silent. As it neared the shore, the sea erupted into a symphony of song and spray, dazzling the eyes and ears of onlookers. Crabs scuttled away. A tall rock, about forty feet high, stood before him, its top almost flat and offering an easy climb.

At its peak, the rocky outcrop offered a breathtaking panorama of the bustling port and its tiny market far below, barely visible on the horizon. Below him, the humble huts of local fishermen dotted the landscape. Male Minoans, clad only in loincloths, perched on the rocks' submerged edges, their eyes fixed on the endless expanse of the Libyan Sea.

Gazing out at the vast sea, one could not help but feel humbled by the sheer scale and beauty of nature, which seemed indifferent to the great affairs of man.

The surf's song arrived as a delicate whisper, much like the sound of the ocean within a seashell. The sun's rays danced upon the water's surface as the waves thundered and crashed upon the shore. A rim of pure white marble seemed to rise from the sea, its crest adorned with a crown of frothy foam. Majestic and powerful, it broke upon the rocks with a resounding thunder.

So luminous and moving was the picture of the breeze-swept sea, the blue sky, and the foam-dashed rocks, a mysterious festival of nature. There were flights of seagulls rising here and there in clouds like small puffs of smoke.

Kyros, a strapping man with skin sun-kissed and rippling with toned muscles honed by years of hard work, trod lightly on the jagged stone chunks along the shore. Standing at the water's edge, he poised his spear with precision, ready to hunt beneath the surface. With a swift thrust, he plunged the spear deep into a swirling pool, emerging moments later with a bountiful catch.

As he basked in the warm Mediterranean sun, he shed his loincloth on a nearby rock and set his spear aside, plunging headfirst into the cool embrace of the sea. With the grace of a dolphin, Kyros dove naked into a deep, tranquil pool, the crystal-clear revealing a hidden world of vibrant marine life.

A world of wonder teeming with life in all its vibrant forms. Shoals of small and large fish darted to and fro, their scales flashing like jewels in the sunlight. Barnacles clung tightly to rocks, while cuttlefish and sea snails roamed the sandy floor below.

Amidst this diverse and colourful marine landscape, globe-shaped jellyfish floated like iridescent orbs, while black sea urchins nestled amidst the crevices of the rocky seabed. Strips of dark seaweed swayed gently in the ebb and flow of the tides, casting an emerald hue upon the waters.

And yet, amidst all this beauty and grace, it was the female sea turtle Kareta that captured the heart. With her sturdy rear flippers, she dug her nest in the sand with care and tenderness, a labour of love that would soon bring forth new life to this enchanted world.

Kyros finally reached the great port market. It was so close to the shore, and its density varied. Honeycombed with cobblestone streets, it had stalls of dry and wet food, large storage vessels, and cliffs of solid vapour, all shifting and changing as locals walked through. Birds clucked. Lots of herbs were neatly tucked next to each other in bundles.

Moments later, Kyros stood in front of a stall full of crisp, pink-orange apples.

'Apples from the birthplace of the Fallen Stars! Get one now or miss your chance!' the owner called out while eating one apple after another.

His wet raven-black hair cascaded down his broad shoulders, framing a sharp gaze that met Petra's with a hint of mischief. With a goofy smile, he greeted her warmly, his eyes crinkling at the corners.

Petra was stunningly beautiful, with a perfectly formed and fully developed figure that belied her youthful age. Despite her looks, she had little patience for joviality in others. Even the sight of Kyros's eyes, with their black circles and friendly smile, irritated her to no end.

As Petra approached Basilios, Kyros watched from a distance, his attention caught by the sight of her basket brimming with apples. He observed her march towards the shoreline, her face twisted with a multitude of expressions born of her frustrated thoughts. There, Basilios rested his bones by the shore alongside two boys who looked to be around his age. A freckled and tanned thirteen-year-old who had the appearance of a young boy but the promise of a fine man. Healthy-looking, with a daring, almost impudent expression.

As Kyros watched, he saw Basilios extend his hand, reaching up towards the sky, casting a shadow on his eyes from the blinding sunlight. A seagull circled around Basilios's view, and Kyros could sense the child's curious mind: the mind of a dreamer.

'Bas! Bas!' Petra shouted, and as she did, Kyros saw the seagull drift gently out to sea. Its cry came mixed with the spray on the breeze, and Basilios sat up, turning in her direction as the water hissed. 'Come take your father off the stall! Or else he'll eat all the apples,' she snapped. 'We won't have any left to sell!'

As they walked hastily towards the market, Kyros saw a poised, broad-shouldered old man approach to inspect the apples.

'Are these really from the Land of the Fallen Stars?' the man asked, frowning.

'L'me tell you, they are as real as I'm standing here right now. Nourished through a rough landscape of dust and rocks. Narrow rockfalls spread out before the vast southern Libyan Sea, on whose opposite shore lie the dark umber people browned by the unforgiving sun. Where the north wind howls down the cliffs, fills the sea with white lambs, and whips up the water into small waterspouts . . . identified by the brilliant, shooting Sagittarius above the sky!'

'Give me a dozen.' The old man paid with a bunch of dark red saffron, a vivid crimson colouring that came as a surprise.

As the man departed with his prized purchase, Kyros plucked an apple from the nearby basket and gestured towards the vibrant saffron with an outstretched hand. 'Did you see that?'

'Great job! Now, leave the apple where you took it from and go help Hyrtacus,' Petra instructed him.

Kyros returned the apple with a sulk and took the role of a fish vendor beside Hyrtacus, as instructed.

Hyrtacus was an old man with many wrinkles and a well-maintained physique, evidence of a warrior's advanced age. He sharpened his knife and chopped fish.

Basilios approached him. 'I think we should sell plane tree leaves,' he said without blinking. Anything other than apples was a taboo subject for Kyros.

'What's wrong with selling what we sell?' asked Kyros, genuinely curious.

'One, you devour the goods we've procured, leaving nothing to sell or to savour. Two, there's nothing wrong with selling apples, but why limit ourselves to fruit alone? I just think it would be more profitable if we expand to plane tree leaves.'

'Why would people buy plane tree leaves?'

'By the shore we sat, my friend and I, and he spoke of his maiden sister's quest. She sent him to Gortys to gather leaves of the plane tree, believing in tales of Zeus in bull form and Europa, his princess fair. Beneath that very tree, they say, he revealed his divine identity and made love to her, blessing her with three sons. And so it is said, these leaves possess powers beyond our knowing, to bless women with sons and keep their spirits glowing. For women, as they age, often grow a little wild, so why not turn a profit?' Basilios explained.

'When did you become a merchant?' Kyros asked his son, his voice full of pride and gruffness as he skilfully cut through the fish, preparing it for sale.

The sun sank into the west. It was nearly an hour or two before sunset, and their apple stall had completely sold out. Kyros had just finished washing his sharp blades in a clay pot when Petra tossed an apple his way. He held out one edge in anticipation, and the apple split in half and dropped onto the empty stall.

'Good reflexes, but I am not trying to attack you,' she said.

Kyros grabbed one of the two pieces and took a bite. 'How do I know?' he said as he munched.

''Cause I would not be using an apple!'

A few feet distant, a woman and her daughter stood before a fruit vendor, making a late purchase. The bald, short, overweight man with a thin dark moustache and beard packed his wares away.

The woman handed him a saffron thread in exchange for a peach, but he rejected the payment, throwing the thread back at her face disrespectfully.

'Get out of here, Damaris!' he shouted.

The port's market was still bustling with a crowd of men and women tidying up, but none reacted. They spectated as if they were standing by just to criticise or approve. Kyros approached, followed by Petra and Basilios.

'What's the problem?' Kyros asked.

'This woman is trying to pass me for a fool! That's the problem!' barked the fruit vendor. He looked at the woman and said, 'I have been browned by the sun and the sea breeze, and I won't trade the fruits of my labour for your old inventory.' The vendor must have looked like a perfect savage, as seen by her daughter, who cried her eyes out.

'Anysia . . . Shush, little one.' Damaris rested a comforting hand on the girl's shoulder as the vendor disappeared.

Kyros bent the knee, offering his remaining apple piece to Anysia, whose tears were halted by his gesture.

'It is not much, and it is not what you wanted . . . but it would make me happy if you accepted this, young girl.'

'We can't accept this. That's too expensive! I can't pay you.' Damaris reacted with panic as her daughter's belly betrayed a soft murmur.

'It is a gift, m'lady.'

As they made their way out of the market, Kyros gave them something to ponder. 'This young girl hadn't eaten in days. Do you think plane tree leaves can bring as much joy as this apple did just now?' He continued, 'Bas, it's not all about profit. One good turn deserves another.'

'That was the last apple you ate for today, by the way,' Petra quipped.

'What do you mean? Am I not allowed one more after my good deed?'

'Absolutely not!'

'Ruthless you are.'

After hours of horse riding and trekking through the dry, unapproachable mountains, Kyros, Basilios, and their small group descended from the rocks and made their way back through the trees. They were headed towards the Land of the Fallen Stars, a pilgrimage site located in a fortified valley behind cliffs of rocks, with passages in and out of the town only down and through that path. It was a fitting name for the community of surviving archers who had settled in this valley after the wars.

Kyros unfastened the leather thong securing his staff to the saddle and turned to check on Hyrtacus. The old man was sitting beside a small settlement, his eyes closed. Kyros knew that Hyrtacus often dreamt of his daughter, Ilya, and wondered if that was also the case now. Hyrtacus had even revealed once in his sleep that he had seen her lie on a bed by a window, with skin as pale as milk and hair like Medea, glowering at him with eyes expressing infinite anger.

As Kyros watched, Hyrtacus's expression grew haunted, and he began to speak in his sleep. 'For survival. A day might come when you turn into prey,' he murmured. Then his dream turned violent, and he twisted and turned, his voice growing louder and more desperate, as if he had been stabbed in the heart.

Kyros shook him awake, calling his name. 'Don't fall asleep here. The vicious mosquitoes will feed on you.'

Rheumy with tears, Hyrtacus nodded and ran a hand across his scalp. 'I drifted off.' He gave the ghastliest look.

'You look like you've seen a ghost. What did you see?'

Hyrtacus stood and slowly made a move towards his home. 'Nothing I want to relive by saying it out loud.'

A few moments later, Kyros and Basilios sat on a boulder near the shore, watching the light of distant stars drift down like mist by a pit fire. The sea and sky were full of stars, and the waning gibbous moon lit and veiled the world in equal measure. The only sound was the majestic thunder of the waves.

Kyros hummed the Song of Seikilos, breaking the silence, the innocence of its melody filling the background. 'As long as you live, shine. Let nothing grieve you beyond measure. For your life is short, and time will claim its toll.' He took a breath, filling his lungs with cold air and letting the light of the stars speak to him. The sea slept underneath, while the Sagittarius constellation hung on the fiery arch of the Milky Way like a broken kite.

'Mother is one of those stars.' Basilios had not spoken of his mother since forever.

'She is . . . and she shines as brightly as the first day I met her. Life is joyful, and she always greeted it with joy,' Kyros said with a hint of nostalgia.

A vast, vague noise echoed from far down the rocks under the night. Kyros rose to its rattling sound.

'What's this noise?' Basilios asked.

Kyros turned to his left, where the sound came from. A goat stood at the top of the cliffside near an apple tree . . . eating an apple.

'Aw no, no, no, noooo . . . ' Kyros's voice ascended.

Basilios chortled at his father.

'Get away from my apples, you snowy ferocious goat.' He launched at it with a small rock, but it quickly side-stepped his attack.

Basilios laughed happily, but his laughter trailed off as the goat ate one more.

'While you're alive, shine,' he sang as his father climbed the rock carefully. 'Never let your mood decline.'

The lyrics swept over them as swiftly as the water caressing the rocks. As Kyros lifted the goat, its scream echoed all the way down.

'We've a brief span of life to spend,' Basilios continued as Kyros left the goat a few feet from the apple tree. It ran and disappeared into the night.

'When time demands an end,' Basilios finished his song that mocked the whole scene.

Kyros climbed back down, puffing, and sat next to his son with a half-eaten apple in his hands.

'Don't tell Petra,' Kyros instructed while finishing the half-eaten fruit.

'It's beyond me how you have the energy of a bull to fight against a goat but cannot argue with Petra . . . over apples!'

'Petra loves me. She just doesn't know it yet.'

'Just marry the poor woman. If anyone can put up with you, it's her.'

As Basilios threw twigs in the pit fire, a dim smile escaped Kyros. This was a familiar feeling he'd lived through before, over and over—when one has contemplated death enough to finally look in the face of reality.

The first time, he was eight. He sat across his mother's deathbed, surrounded by the sounds of the bedwarmers and former slaves of the pleasure house that catered to erotic tastes. A brothel, dirtier than most, where a man could enjoy a woman without fear of being at a disadvantage of some sort.

Kyros grew up there, clinging to his mother's skirt. A grace, one she'd earned through whoring. A girl of noble birth who was too young to have served her years in a pleasure house. Her family fragmented when her father left for war. She was taken from her home by raiders and sold into slavery.

Young as she was, Ilya had shown such a gift of eloquence that the raiders put it to use. She was armoured only in her innocence when she was first brought there. Paid to play with every highborn in the city for gold, which eventually helped her raise a noble bastard.

He was too young, but he knew slaves were everywhere, as numerous as cockroaches, scurrying about their business, with the plumpest ones being the hungriest and loudest abed. This was his home, the place where the only person he cared about lived. But now, the most beautiful woman whom he held so dear was in front of him, lifeless on a mattress stuffed with straw in this small bedchamber.

Kyros refused to abandon her. Her death proved to be the catalyst that led to grief. Three daybreaks passed. The room smelled of death. He was on the brink of dying from dehydration and famine, and all he could do was stare at her cadaverous face while contemplating. *Was it a good thing being born?*

False reasoning developed. Reality was harsh, and he did not have the answers. He couldn't have known this was how his mother would die.

That was when Hyrtacus appeared. He looked like a true and chivalrous knight, and he took his helping hand like a drowning child grasping at a straw. Was his sudden appearance the catalyst that led to a life sentence? Hyrtacus provided water and pressed an old, dried apple into his hands. It was small and withered, but one that set him right.

Just as he ate the whole thing, Hyrtacus asked, 'Are you the creature that came forth from her womb?'

He was not wrong, Kyros thought, shivering, but he held his silence. 'What's your name?'

'Kyros. Just Kyros.'

Hyrtacus wrapped him to keep him warm and paid his daughter a long stare. Kyros understood enough to get the gist. They were both mourning.

'Your mother is dead, and the deceased are but forgotten souls. Do you know why?' With tears streaming down his face, he uttered a sombre truth—that only in death can life find its worth.

Only in death can life find its worth? Kyros wrapped his arms around himself. The death of his kin poisoned his mind, already swirling in negative thoughts.

'Don't be sad. I am sure, for her, her death was a blessed relief. In life, the gods make arrangements before one's passing, and their decree guarantees an afterlife. Your mother will be reborn, and when she is, she will need goods. What do you say? Will you help me with her funeral?' Hyrtacus asked with a courtesy that made Kyros's mouth ache.

Hyrtacus wrapped Ilya's dead body in a tunic and took it in his arms.

As they left this small bedchamber, Kyros asked, 'Who are you?'

Hyrtacus's shattered heart replied, 'I am Hyrtacus. Just Hyrtacus.'

They carried her body to Maleme, and the trip took several daybreaks. When Kyros asked him about his connection to his mother, he said he'd known her family. They occasionally took breaks at taverns to keep warm and well-fed.

Sometimes, they would eat broth that smelled of eggs, tomatoes, onions, and celery. Other times, it would be a fisherman's broth that smelled of the catch of the day, garlic, onion, and leek. Aromatic smells and flavours were enough to fill their belly.

'I lost my family while in the king's service and am now just a deserter. But you have the right to cherish a future better than mine. The choice is yours. Are you going to be a slave and die abed like your mother? If not, come with me and be your own master. I'll teach you the skills you need to survive, and I'll even teach you how to read and write. And when you are old enough, you'll be your own lord. As long as you are alive, you'll figure it out,' Hyrtacus said in a moment of weakness during one of those meals.

'I would like that.'

'No one ever kept me safe when I was little. But I will protect you.'

Days later, Ilya's body was placed in the burial chamber where her mother and siblings were interred.

'Your boy will be safe, Ilya. I will raise him under my protection. I promise,' he swore.

While looking for a place to call home, Hyrtacus showed Kyros how to hunt and butcher a carcass, how to fish and bone, how to find his way through the woods and retrace his steps. Slowly, the apprentice became the master, and during the hours of rest, Hyrtacus revealed more than he'd wished to. He tossed for hours through his nightmares and wept and pleaded for forgiveness, letting slip that Ilya was his daughter.

Is this what reality sounds like? Kyros thought. He had no sympathy for strangers, but for his family, he did. He understood the disgrace and desolation of his heart, so he never revealed he knew the truth. It would only add pressure and guilt to an already broken man. This was a grim reality, and each had his own demons to battle.

Years later came the second. The bells rang at the birth of Kyros's child. It was during the month of Basilios when he was brought to her.

Grievously wounded from childbirth and near death, his wife urged him to take care of the child. He stared at her, now at the gates of the Underworld, as she pleaded to name him.

'What about Basilios?' he asked. A special time they spent together when the son they loved was born. Both took that as an omen.

'I like that name,' she said with a voice as soft as silk. 'Basilios.' She gave her newborn one last glance and said, 'It was an honour to meet you.' Their helpless, sulking baby cried by her deathbed as Kyros weep-watered Gaia. He became a widower and a father within the same month.

The life he had imagined was stolen in a heartbeat. He secretly wished he could freeze or burn death as the day darkened, like his heart. Death filled Gaia, and it was overbearing. The room smelled of blood and ruin, but also of hope, a power stronger than death itself.

Kyros felt alone and lost, but only one look at his newborn gave him the will to move on for his sake. He desperately wanted a family of his own, yet he feared he was not ready when the gods took her away. He blamed himself. One thing was clear: her death and Basilios's birth were all related. He felt it in his gut. They were specks of dust at the gods' fingertips. That was the grim reality that had remained clouded to him for a while.

May the gods take pity on her soul and let her pass the Elysian Fields, he prayed.

Years passed until his son was old enough to ask why his mother was dead. Kyros hid his face as he reflected bitterly.

'She had fought bravely to bring you to this world, but lost the battle. The gods gave her only one child, and you were enough. She loved you with all her strength till the very end. She felt content.'

Basilios assumed a degree of responsibility for her death when he said, 'Was it good that I was born? If I weren't, this wouldn't have happened.'

The lad and he were one and the same. After that day, the conversations about his mother were short to non-existent. One child dared to say that Basilios had murdered his mother, and the thoughts cast shadows for years.

A wonderful night filled with all the majesty and beauty of starlight, and he knew—this was the moment they both moved on.

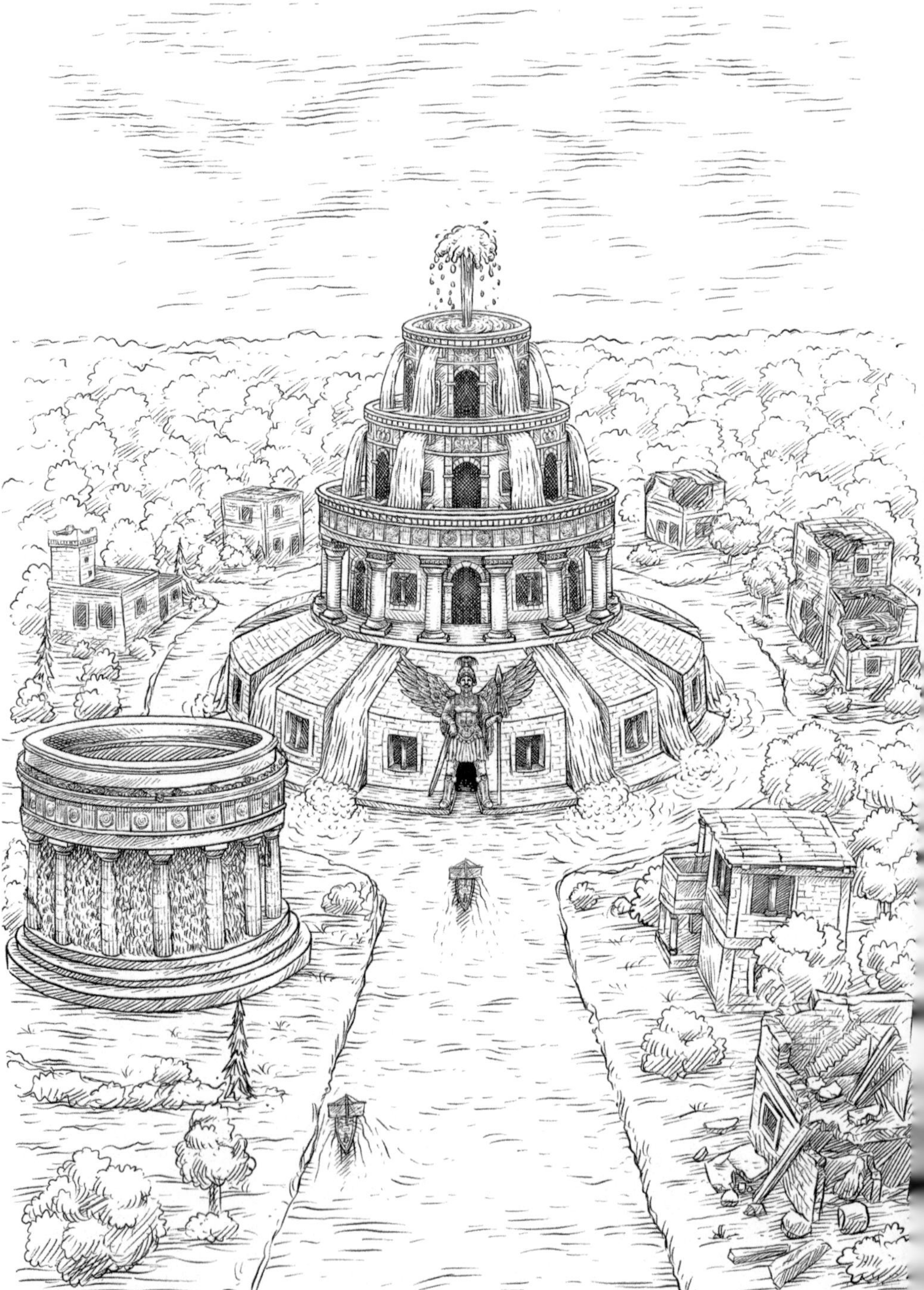

ERIS

Perched atop a branch, Eris, the goddess of chaos, watched as a pale spectral light fell diagonally upon the grass, where a goddess lay surrounded by flowers and all the kindliness of nature. Clotho. She was born a Fate, and together with her sisters, they assured the triumph of death. She had hundreds of thousands of epithets, but she'd forgotten most of them. She had never paid much attention to them.

In fact, she made no special effort to learn them. The epithets faded and were lost in the mists of time. New voices would appear to fashion her names of their own: The Life-Giver, The Spindle Bearer, The Spinner. The summons was usually pulled through heavy breathing and came in the hour before a child's birth when the world stood still and grey. She, of necessity, the one who spun the thread of human life. Her parents had named her Clotho, and the air hung heavy around her when summoned, like chains jangling softly.

Glossy blue-black strands framed her youthful and innocent face, and a long dress covered her fair skin. A bunch of flowers and foliage set in the midst of the blowing wind. She observed a withered flower whose stalk was slightly cut. In her solitude, the flower was carefully tended. Her lips kissed the dying flower, breathing life into it.

'This will be our secret,' she whispered, and then a summons echoed within the forest like the sound of a hundred women in labour, anguished and loud. Clotho slowly stood. She turned into a phoenix and set herself on fire, vanishing along with her ashes.

At that moment, Menoetius appeared from thin air. He bent over and cut that same flower. He placed it on his lips and suavely kissed it, as if to steal away that kiss. His eyes swept over a black raven that kept watch over him. It observed his every move in cold suspicion.

Menoetius did not like the strangeness of that bird. It had dull white eyes, and its flank was translucent from its throat to the belly. Its blood vessels resembled the black-coloured branches of trees. Yet, it was oddly familiar. Was it madness that seized him? He was the titan of rash violence, after all. Was it some wisdom buried in his blood? Menoetius looked at the bird, dropped the flower, and disappeared.

Eris's disdain for Menoetius could only be rivalled by his for her. Even through the eyes of her ever-loyal raven, she could not bear the sight of him. The goddess's thoughts were suddenly brought to a halt by the sound of a boat crossing the narrow river nearby. The surface of the River Styx was so still that the chuckling of the water at the boat's bow could be heard distinctly as it drove forward under the impetus of the last powerful strokes. The oarsman and the boat's passenger were hidden beneath full-body hooded cloaks, and only small portions of their body were exposed to the public eye.

Not that anyone was around to see, or at least so they thought. The light here allowed the onlooker to see the loveliness of the forest, the green of the trees, all sharply outlined. Coloured and arrogant, yet tender, heartbreakingly beautiful. A strange place.

Here, the green of the weeds was lighter, and there, darker. The vegetation had burst into a colourful riot. All sorts of sappy stalks of unknown plants barred the way. The reason: Titan Atlas's daughters had taken root in, descending from the light to rob and kill whenever someone rode out in search of their kind.

Atlantis lay near the island of Crete, where the shadows leapt and danced behind the great Minoan Empire. Who had seen a shadow separated from the light? It blew in the dark with the nymphs and spirits that prowled these forests. The Hesperides, with their violet eyes and long, dark copper hair that reached their waists, were said to appear only at sunset, emerging from the shadows like deer.

Hyades and Pleiades were armoured, with light-brown hair curled in a plait on one side or worn as a crown, and eyes dark as amber. They stirred beneath rain and clouds as easily as if their element were a suit of clothes tailored to their bodies. Around these places, the woods were thicker than elsewhere, hinting at the presence of those divine creatures. The idols were immense, their faces vague. The winds, the river, and the trees of the ages had cast over them a veil.

Atlas's daughters were the pillars of Atlantis, while the naiads, dryads, and aurae were its soul. The aurae were nymphs of the breezes, with white hair and large blue eyes. One nymph had a golden complexion and a beautiful summer face that shone like the sun. Another was as cold and dry as the winter air, with an icy demeanour that could chill even the warmest hearts.

Under them loomed no signs of habitation but the mournful and perpetual buzz of insects that filled the silence without destroying it. The old oarsman and his companion rowed a few strokes. The river was about to split in half.

In the middle lay a block-shaped stone of Mount Ida, a sentinel old, hewn and honed, its surface marked with Linear A glyphs in curling script. The words they read, a warning dire: *'Anyone who enters must adhere to rules that govern this sacred ground, and should you stray, you may be bound.'* Its message was clear: beware and fear.

Such was the might of these rocks, imbued with the power to commune with Mother Earth. Their wandering eyes roved over the right, where a massive wooden double door stood tall, covered by a thick blanket of twigs and vines. Raging water flew over the entrance. From somewhere in the dark came the gruesome sound of bones snapping and flesh ripping.

A vast, vague swell lifted the undulations to the rattling sound of the gate points and the occasional creak of the chains that held the door shut. A vast expanse of rippling cerulean water extended in all directions, as far as the eye could see, flanking the boat's sides. Calm with the tints of sapphire. As a faint sound came from the river, the oarsman paused on his oars. Vicious twigs appeared from the bottom of the boat, lifting it upwards and bringing it to a halt.

As they gazed ahead, the sight unfolded, sprouting forth into dryads, veering towards the right. Ethereal beings, their tresses dyed in emerald hues, enrobed in boughs of green mould. Wise women of yore, guardians of these woods and mountain peaks, ageless and revered.

The land now swelled with verdant hills, and amidst it all, a naiad appeared. A spirit with locks of raven dye and eyes that mirrored the rivers and streams she called her home. A woman of some ancient years who moved with grace and poise, her form beguilingly youthful, lean, and lithe. Adorned with tendrils and tentacles akin to creatures of the sea, she wore a hat that seemed to sway like a jellyfish in the tide. With her sinewy appendages, she subdued the passenger, unravelling the cloak that hid their face.

'What madness is this? Your actions inflict harm upon your queen!' the oarsman roared more loudly than he'd intended.

Lofty was the rank of the passenger, the spouse to King Minos. Who would have thought that Queen Pasiphae would rise from her throne and be dragged here to explore the depths of chaos? Was she given a choice?

At the sound of his words, the naiad raised her gaze to him. She studied the trembling oarsman, rife with fear. 'I answer to no queen!' she declared with a voice thick as the river's flow.

The queen's peachy skin welcomed a petulant smile, which twitched at her small mouth. 'Please, I come bearing gifts.' These few words made the rustic gods smile at her.

The naiad uncoiled her tendrils, releasing Pasiphae from their grip. With arms stretched, Pasiphae proffered a bundle wrapped in a tunic. Its contents were soon exposed: two human hearts, bloodied and hidden within. The naiad stared at her quizzically.

'Two lives for two lives,' Pasiphae stated, firm in her conviction. The naiad's voice rang out, stern yet exultant, directing them to the left. With a jolt, Pasiphae awoke from her daze as the dryad set the boat free in the river's flow.

The boat set sails to the left of the river, and, heartbeats later, a dimly lit forest appeared through the mist. The boat's figure came out from amidst the distant trees on the other side of the sward. The oarsman puffed and blew, his cheeks ballooning like twin orbs as he tugged at the oars.

The boat loomed nearer a water metropolis built on top of a previous sunken city, on a group of small islands separated by the River Styx and linked by earthen bridges. At its heart stood a grand edifice, its form that of a monumental fountain, its tiers stretching high, from where waterfalls tumbled down with a melodious sigh. Adorned with a statue of Amphiaraus at its entrance, resembling an angelic deity wielding a sword. As the waterfalls gurgled and whispered, the oarsman pulled the boat onto the opposite shore outside a shrine and secured it in place with deft skill.

Before the shrine's door, the oarsman sat, worn out and exhausted, when Pasiphae knocked upon it. Its columns were fashioned from Helidon sandstone, and blooming vines adorned the spaces between, forming walls both thick and lush. Mystery shrouded all within the temple of Eris, illuminated only by the soft glow of entwined wood candles that burnt together.

She, of strife and discord, was depicted with a visage both youthful and deceitful, framed by flowing tresses of silver-grey, injected with crimson blood. Her gaze fixed upon the bowl of destiny, while one eye remained closed. Within the glass vessel swirled the tears of giants, containing knowledge of fate and the future, so potent that even a single glance could reveal all that lay ahead.

A raven, obsidian in hue, with white eyes devoid of life, alighted upon Eris's outstretched palm. In a flash of magic, the raven transformed into a glassy black orb akin to the eyes of a drunkard. Eris took the eye and placed it within her left socket. As the injected blood drained from her face, it coalesced within the eye, then vanished.

KNOCK, KNOCK, KNOCK. The knocker clanged loud but as expected.

'Come, child,' Eris said, without turning away from her business.

The door cracked, spilling shallow light onto Pasiphae. The woman who stepped through the door was no longer a queen, but an anxious and worried mother. She closed the door behind her and swiftly approached the goddess.

Upon her knees, Pasiphae spoke with awe and reverence; her words echoed like a sacred prayer. She clasped Eris's hand with both hands and placed it on her forehead, a gesture of her utmost devotion. 'Oh, divine harbinger of disorder and creation, you have graced me with your presence and heard my voice,' she whispered, her gratitude and overwhelming sense of appreciation for the goddess's divine favour ringing clear in every syllable.

Eris smiled as if nothing gave her greater pleasure. 'Stand up, child.'

Pasiphae rose to her feet, but her words were heavy with a sense of foreboding. 'I come bearing gifts to pay my respects and show my gratitude,' she implored, extending her arms, the bundle within the tunic cradled gently. But as the queen drew nearer to the scary demon before her, a surge of fear took hold, causing her to retreat, her heart heavy with dread.

Eris placed the tunic on the table and gingerly unfurled its contents. A crimson rivulet trickled out from a bat's heart, staining the fabric in a macabre display.

'When the first light of dawn breaks and the morning breeze drifts in from the sea, your husband will be crowned king of the island,' Eris proclaimed, a pleased smile spreading across her face. With a final glance at the bat, she pondered all the ways its bones could serve her. 'Now, go forth and celebrate your hard-won victory.'

Pasiphae stood still, the weight of some unspoken worry bearing heavily upon her. 'My Goddess, as a mortal mother to the mother of chaotic creation, I humbly seek one final boon from thee,' she entreated, her voice laden with reverence and trepidation.

She peered with the same worried expression she had worn since the moment she'd stepped through the door.

'Asterion is not the monster they make him out to be,' the queen spoke with unapologetic grief. 'He is bound to feed on humans, for he knows nothing else.'

Eris was no stranger to Asterion, for he was a true guardian of chaos. A Boopis creature, with the head of a white bull and the body of a man. She had seen his muscular physique before, dewdrops shimmering upon his rippled, sinewy muscles as he was rounding the labyrinth's blood-drenched ground.

A long-deserted room, where the spirits of the dead manned his loneliness. No human lived there. At least not for too long, as they were always ridden in deadly danger. Only the ghosts skirted his underground prison and moaned among the stone columns.

He fed on the flesh of the dead like a bearded vulture. Cold things, dead things, who couldn't drink themselves jovially into oblivion. They illustrated the futility of one's own fight against the looming spectre of death. Unremembered casualties in the inglorious labyrinth. Some gave up much more quickly than others, trembling and soiling themselves in fear.

Amidst puddles of blood, they lay, their hatred for the gods and every creature with ichor in their veins forever silenced. Lost in Lethe's embrace, they were doomed to oblivion. And yet, the goddess of oblivion watched on, triumphantly observing his work, for she alone understood the significance of his tasks and how they elevated her power. He rode atop their pale, dead corpses, unfeeling and pitiless.

A child of shame, but with a higher purpose. His very breath was a gift from the gods. His presence, a sentence of death. For years, he searched for the exit until he despaired of ever finding the way out. He was an illegitimate creature who would never have a legitimate claim to the things that others had. Things such as love, family, home, and acceptance.

He didn't want immortality. He wanted reality. A future. But the marks humans left him with were scars. He had become a heartbroken hell-raiser whose only personal connection was with corpses. A heart of chaos beat inside his chest, growing strong and powerful by the minute.

Their interests aligned, for his wrath fuelled her children's immortality. He was a creature of terror, feared by the living. Atë, swift-footed and chaotic, treaded on Asterion's head, wreaking havoc and delusion. Painful Ponos fed on the toil and hardship of his victims, followed by Limos, the insatiable devourer of emptiness.

Limos filled the void of her stomach with the hybrid's unquenchable appetite, driving him to prey upon humans. Her scaly throat coated in scurf, she would yank it loose, leaving her sister Algea to feast upon the victim's physical and mental pain. Meanwhile, Asterion devoured extracted limbs before the flies came, occasionally defiling a lifeless body here and there.

The thought would make a normal person sick. But Eris was no normal person. She of strife and discord found this perfect and beautiful. She of chaos found this heart-breaking but romantic. *There is nothing more beautiful than death*, she thought.

The seeds of tragedy he sowed in people's lives laid the foundation of her children's glory. Each time he fulfilled a wish of his heart, someone else's dream was shattered or embraced, a reminder of the order of things. His deeply ingrained lack of love made him who he was. He took whatever love the victims had in their hearts, even consuming the heart itself to transfer the affection from whomever they loved to himself. He controlled and kept them with him for as long as possible.

'I am aware of the situation. Minos is just using him to bring fear and dread to his enemies.'

Amidst the flickering candles, Eris listened intently while peering deep into the bowl of destiny. Within its murky depths, she saw a vision of the future she dreaded most: a slain Minotaur at the hands of a foreign foe, a threat to the very essence of chaos itself. How could she allow a mere mortal to steal away the momentum of anarchy?

'He is my son, imprisoned and unwillingly bearing the weight of my past sins,' Pasiphae spoke with deadly earnestness, her heart heavy with pain.

To Eris, Pasiphae's attempts to protect the innocence of her brutal and bloodthirsty son seemed futile. However, she understood the need to find meaning in one's past, to hold on to the hope that the years had not been meaningless.

'My husband tells me he needs to stay imprisoned . . . because mortals always fear the things they don't understand and draw forth the most exquisite visions of terror.' Pasiphae continued, 'He says if he is freed, death will be his fate.'

As Pasiphae's eyes grew watery, Eris stared mournfully at the bowl of destiny. 'A time shall come when the sun sets, and the warm amber glow of the sunset will cast its light upon the rocks of the island to witness Asterion forfeiting his life before a man.'

Pasiphae's voice caught in her throat, a silent scream bubbling within her. She longed to let it out, to cry out against the Fates that had brought her to this moment. But all that escaped her lips was a faint, mournful whisper. 'Nooooo . . .'

Something gave an edge to the scene as baffling shadows thrown by the flickering candles filled the shrine. Something was about to happen.

'But . . . I am chaos. I am the spirit with which your children and mine laugh in happy anarchy. As long as I exist, I can delay the grasp of the Fates' inflexible claws that seek to claim him.'

Heartbeats later, the oarsman guided Pasiphae onto the boat. Towering over Eris, Titan Menoetius fixed her with a piercing gaze as she sought answers within the mystical bowl of destiny.

'Giants' tears,' Menoetius said. 'Whom did you make cry? Enceladus? Etna? Porphyrion, perhaps?' He named all the giants who came to mind.

'Ponos is wonderful,' Eris said, bragging while switching gears.

'A parent always praises their child.' Menoetius's taunts had been the loudest.

'Weren't you playing hide-and-seek with your love just now? Why are you here?'

Menoetius gently touched the bat's skin; his fingertips came away red. 'You can feel it there, like a fever.'

'She wakes me . . . nourishes me. She reminds me how sweet the suffering of mortals tastes,' Eris retorted happily, the corners of her lips curling upwards.

'Next time, choose a mortal who is not among my worshippers for your schemes.' Menoetius let his remark fly as quickly as Zeus's thunderbolts without pausing for an answer.

Eris could sense his disapproval, knowing that he had uncovered her actions. She had instructed her daughter, Atë, to tread on his minion's head, wreaking havoc and delusion, in order to steal gold from the king's party, whom the young heir subsequently killed. Such a heinous act would also serve to feed her son, Phonoi. It was a scheme crafted to push Erythrus's legitimacy closer to claiming the throne while simultaneously leveraging Minos up and causing Menoetius to fall behind, killing three birds with one stone.

'I am sorry! Do you miss your *thief?*' Eris's cackle rose, her laughter mocking him.

'He stole them for me . . . as an offering.' His explanation brought more guffaws from Eris.

'I make the world a better place by leading it my way.'

As the flickering flame danced before him, Menoetius spoke. 'Danger excites you. And as you well know, I am dangerous. Action and power will draw you like a moth to a flame.' His gaze shifted, meeting Eris's own. 'But mark my words, should you ever again use Atë and Phonoi to do your bidding on my advocates, I will not hesitate to parade their cold, lifeless bodies from every corner of Gaia and feed their souls to the vilest filth in Tartarus.'

Eris eyed Menoetius keenly. 'You are your father's son and a great titan indeed . . . but with such an impulsive tongue of violent anger and rashness,' she growled. 'Do you truly believe you can barge into my sacred shrine and threaten the lives of my beloved children?'

'I am a titan, and I ABHOR your insolence—'

'And I am chaos,' she quipped.

'If passing on my cruelty and rage upon your children is what it takes to get through to you, then so be it.'

'As such, I will rain down upon you every agony and violation imaginable . . . upon your family as well. This is what happens when you set yourself up for the brazier. Your life will be robbed. Consider this my promise.' Eris challenged his gaze.

Thousands of feet away from Eris's shrine stood the walled chamber of the Fates, a fortress of stone and streams of water atop a three-tiered fountain. The black raven, with eyes like winter snow, drew in closer to the towering statues that encircled the courtyard, each a representation of the sisters of Fate.

Clotho's statue depicted an angelic deity with wings and a handbell, while Lachesis's portrayed an angelic deity with open arms. Atropos's statue, on the other hand, depicted an angelic deity wearing a helm, wielding a flagellation whip in one hand and a trumpet-like horn in the other. But at the centre stood Lachesis herself, the measurer of the thread spun on Clotho's spindle.

Peachy-pink undertones framed her youthful, oriental face, her eyes the colour of a pit viper. She wore a long dress draped over her supple skin. A single strand of water wended its way around Lachesis's hands, and above her shoulder, Eris saw Clotho pacing towards her.

'Will you keep this man a celibate to the end of his days?' Clotho inquired.

'I guess you are just not used to this much excitement, sis.' Lachesis smirked as Clotho's very existence was about life creation. As she spun each life's thread, her span grew short. She'd be reborn like the phoenix she was, with visions more severe than others. But her visions of this soul were different.

Who had meddled with his path? Eris wondered if this was what Clotho thought.

'His actions demand the strictest sanctions. He must pay in blood. Atropos just needs to decide how,' Lachesis said.

'I pray he finds peace at last.'

Words of hope were on Clotho's lips, but little did the divine sisters know of Eris's determination to tamper with the order of things.

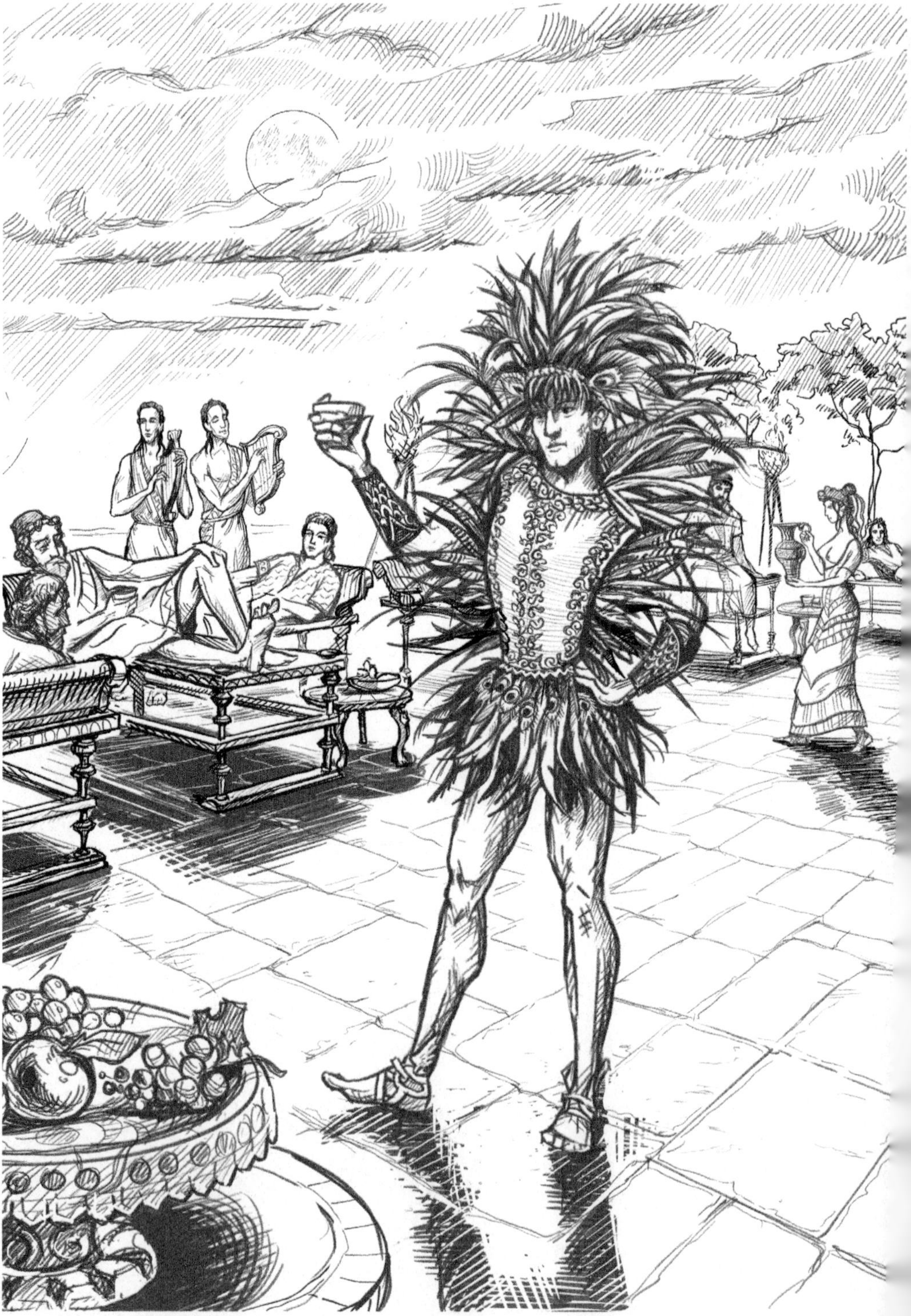

ERYTHRUS

The sun set over the palace's majestic entrance, transforming it into a dazzling spectacle. The ever-loyal raven of Eris swooped down behind the court, where Erythrus fixed his gaze upon a woman standing near the top of the stairs by the Lustral Basin.

Confident in her own skin, her naked figure disappeared into the sunken rectangular tub as he studied her. The setting sun silhouetted the walls of the basin, intricate and colourful geometric patterns decorating the domes.

In the tub, a cheerful woman smiled as she took another's hair and, with her fingers, toyed and whisked it with affection. Two seductive women, dressed in palatial garments, crouched on the pilaster of the tub by a column, playing Zatrikion and merrily refilling the tub when necessary.

Yet Erythrus seethed with anger, his heart heavy with bitterness, as he watched the women play, their carefree manner only heightening his vexation. Heartbeats later, he raced up the steps of the palace, a reticent Meleagros hot on his trail, struggling to keep up.

'Yesterday, the men served Rhadamanthys, the king of Crete. My father, whose place now is in Boeotia! Here comes the morrow, and they serve Minos. His brother,' Erythrus ranted.

'Not his brother,' Meleagros puffed. 'His great-nephew. Your first cousin, Your Grace.'

'His abomination is no kin to me,' Erythrus hissed, his frustration palpable. They raced past an open door, and Erythrus signalled for a drink. After the drink was poured, he slid out of sight down the hallway.

'I am his heir! The rightful king!' Erythrus growled.

'You are still king of Phaestus, Your Grace,' Meleagros tried to calm his spirit.

'Yes . . . but not of this island!'

Sober, Erythrus drank, but a drunken and sullen Erythrus pulled out hours later, mingling with the distant roar of musical strolls of lyre and mandolin that pierced the air. The moon's pale glow cast an ethereal light upon the milling guests. Burning torches illuminated their faces with a warm, flickering flame. A ring of armed Minoans stood guard on foot, their shields, helmets, and sword hilts emblazoned with the personal seal of their owner.

'Amidst the chaos of battle, I have led charges with the sound of my name echoing through the fray. I have vanquished mightier foes and tasted the fleeting elixir of glory, savouring every precious drop. A proven warrior, that's *me*. Not Minos. Yet, I was not good enough for him. All

Minos did was usurp my father. A heartbeat more, and he might have chosen a mummer as his heir.'

'A heartbeat less, and if you usurped him, you might have been the king of Crete today.' Meleagros was a master of Erythrus's rhythmical drunkenness.

'My people need strength, not sentiment.'

'Yet, with all you've done and seen, the prospect of another battle still makes your blood run scorching hot.' Meleagros patted his shoulder. 'Give your wounds time to close.'

'Mummers! Where are the mummers? Mummers are the next best thing to wine,' he whispered to Meleagros, who was not one for fancy mummer shows.

Erythrus lifted his cup, pouring wine just below the brim, and drank. Loaves of hot bread and massive wheels of cheese filled the tables. There were fruits, leeks, carrots, roasted onions, beets, turnips, parsnips, and walnut cakes.

Smoke wafted into the night. Animals roasted, smoked pork chops tended by multiple Minoan men with outsized black moustaches. From the seas came barnacles, cuttlefish, and sea snails. From the land came goats, sheep, hares, pigs, and cattle. All above fire pits and then loaded onto trays. A hundred dishes were served along with rakomelo. Among them, the curved horns of goats decorated the tables.

Kyros and Petra, stalwart Minoans, served the feast's attendees with skill and grace. Apollodorus, though his belly was full, heaved the wine up and gulped it down once more. A smiley, doe-eyed woman approached him, her hands offering a cup filled with dark red wine. He drank deeply, though his head swam, retching and wiping his mouth, yet still, he drank on, seeking solace in the sweet nectar of the gods.

When the last course was served and cleared, the female attendees amazed the crowd with acrobatic headstands, their bodies twisting and turning with nimble grace around a figure hidden behind the mask of the fierce bull. The onlookers cheered with barks of laughter, joyfully applauding the display. Fine steel daggers were bestowed upon their fathers, a symbol of strength and honour. Bolts of silk were gifted to their mothers, a symbol of beauty and grace.

Amidst the revelry, a mighty bull made a grand entrance, its power restrained yet palpable. Titan Epimetheus stood witness to the festivities, his gaze transfixed by the spectacle. As he watched, his brother Menoetius approached with a curious expression, drawn in by the vibrant energy of the festivity.

'Prometheus assigned you with giving the creatures of the earth qualities,' Menoetius spat, his voice heavy with contempt, as the bull's restraints fell away. The animal's vaulter acted recklessly, drawing a disapproving glance from Menoetius. 'What happened?' Passing a wine cup, he offered it to Epimetheus, who gladly took it and drank.

'All the good qualities are out there. None are left for them.'

'You can still carry out the deed Prometheus has asked you to perform.' Menoetius had Epimetheus's attention. 'A drop of blood'—he gestured at the wine cup—'is all it takes.'

Epimetheus chuckled. 'What nonsense do you speak, brother? I couldn't. If I did, then they would be our equals.'

'And if they were, they would be swift and cunning as lighting, strong like a rock! Aren't those the qualities Prometheus wanted you to give?'

With a brave step, the vaulter closed in on the bulls, his hands taking hold of the mighty horns. In one swift motion, he harnessed the beast's strength, springing upward to soar above its goring head. The crowd held their breath as he spun mid-air, his body an elegant blur against the night sky. With a soft thud, he landed on the ground behind the bull, his form as graceful as a bird alighting on a branch.

'And if I fail?'

'Then they will *all* be part of this ritual.' Menoetius's eyes shone with malice.

With one swift, smooth flick of the dagger, the male vaulter slit the bull's throat. Hot, steamy blood poured out. As Epimetheus disappeared into the crowd, Menoetius morphed into Goddess Eris.

Amidst the king's epochal ritual, a celebration of treasure hunt plays and romantic dances, Kyros and Petra twirled in the glow of torchlight, watched by the hundreds. Erythrus stood on the sidelines, a silent observer.

'Would you honour me with this dance, m'lady?' Kyros asked.

Petra nodded and offered her arm. They whisked away to the floor.

'Has anyone told you what a wonderful dancer you are?'

Petra smiled, her dimples gleaming. 'You're very kind. But I would be careful if I were you. People might think you're trying to seduce a free woman.'

'If one dares to seduce an unbetrothed free maiden, ten staters shall he pay. Such a price is worthy.'

'Surely you jest, for if one bears witness—'

'M'lady,' Kyros interrupted, 'may the gods bless us with a long life and let them bear witness to the day we wed.'

Her expression was one of surprise, and he gently brushed the back of his hand against her cheek.

'Basilios needs a mother's embrace, and I, a wife. With hope in my heart, may we dance once more as husband and wife.' With the final note of the song, Kyros gently withdrew.

Epimetheus drew a knife, and with a swift slash, his palm bled into the large krater of wine.

His blood mingled with the crimson liquid, and as he muttered a prayer, he raised his hands and blessed the wine, its potency heightened by his divine benediction.

'This, the ancient gift bestowed upon me, now becomes my flesh and blood, a new covenant to all who partake. Remember me through this wine and let the qualities it imparts be proclaimed until Hades robs you of them.'

Kyros stumbled and collided with Talus, his wine cup shattering on the ground.

'Forgive me, m'lord. I shall fetch another,' Kyros slurred apologetically.

Erythrus rose to his feet, lifting his wine cup in a toast. 'Today, we celebrate a new king for this island. All across the kingdoms, men and women lift toasts to his health. Minoans, drink with me. Your king commands it. To his health!'

The crowd echoed his words, lifting their wine cups to their lips, but the taste that filled their mouths was not wine. Drakon blood, thick and viscous, it delivered a stinging sensation to the back of one's throat. Liquor dripped down Erythrus's chin into his black beard. He flicked it with a forefinger, then licked the finger clean.

'Why aren't you drinking, Meleagros? Are you going to dishonour your king?'

'I have no wine left in my cup, Your Grace.'

Erythrus, drunk and jolly, seized a servant and filled Meleagros's cup to the brim. He then forced wine down his throat. The liquid burnt like fire as it trickled down his gullet, but Erythrus urged him on with a cruel grip, determined to see him drink to the last drop.

'That's it, Meleagros, gulp it down.'

Meleagros coughed and sputtered, struggling to keep the wine down. 'If my lord is pleased now, I must go and find . . . my bed.'

Erythrus laughed and signalled his approval.

At Erythrus's court, Kyros stepped between the chaises, the wine jug held aloft like a precious offering. With practiced ease, he filled Talus's cup to the brim, and the nobleman gulped it down.

'How does it taste, m'lord?' Kyros asked.

'Its truth surpasses that of all the gods of the earth,' Talus replied, savouring the rich flavour. 'Why aren't you having some?'

'We, who serve at your side, are not allowed to drink.'

Talus retrieved the wine jug from Kyros and filled his cup once more, a gesture of conviviality and camaraderie.

'In lands beyond east of Asia, the sharing of wine cups is a symbol of fellowship and kinship,' Talus remarked, extending the cup to Kyros.

'And how did you learn of such customs, m'lord?'

'I make sure I know where the fruits of my labour travel to.' He picked another cup and said, 'Drink, my friend, 'cause you are a brother, not a servant.'

Kyros and Talus, brothers in arms, exchanged cups and toasted their friendship. They locked eyes, and with each sip, their bond grew stronger.

The yard was full of music spilling through. Suddenly, a mummer approached Erythrus's table, clad in a flamboyant costume of peacock feathers. He drank wine and performed a silly act, only to cough up a cone of fire. Erythrus's face reflected caution and distrust, but not fear.

Yet, before the celebrations could resume, the clang of a wine jug shattered the festive atmosphere as a woman's screams ripped through the air. A noble's body, covered in steel scales, appeared abruptly, finding Erythrus fettered in frozen time. Eris materialised, enveloped in a light mist wraith, and draped her arms across his shoulders.

'You had always been fighting for the king's seat. You were going to conquer the world, and then—you were going to rule—the perfect way to bring order out of chaos. And you were doing *very*, very well. Till this happened.' She surveyed the guests, her eyes sharp and knowing. 'Equally strong. More disciplined. Perhaps with the courage to cast you down and take all you hold dear.'

'And who are you?' Erythrus demanded.

'The right question is, who are *they*, drinking the gifts of the gods?'

'What do you mean?'

'Sacrifice them to the titan of violent anger and escape his wrath or die along with them.'

And with those words, Eris quickly disappeared, leaving the flow of time to return to normal. Erythrus felt a fever rising in him and the taste of blood in his mouth as he rose from his chair, deep in thought.

'Cretan soldiers, seize every man and woman. Harm no one but those who resist. For Titan Menoetius!' Erythrus bellowed, his eyes glinting with a cruel delight.

Dozens of intimidating, grizzled Cretan soldiers with rippling muscles charged ahead, each clad in bronze armour, wielding swords, spears, and round shields. Erythrus smirked wickedly and led the way with a slow, taunting approach. He palmed a dagger and threw it straight through the mummer's heart.

As the guests fled in terror, a soldier seized Kyros, but he evaded with agility and rammed the soldier with his shield, knocking him down. He grabbed Talus by the hand, and both ran away from the chaos.

The clang of swords and battle cries echoed through the air as more soldiers followed Erythrus's lead, their eyes piercing with ruthless determination through the crowd.

Printed in Great Britain
by Amazon